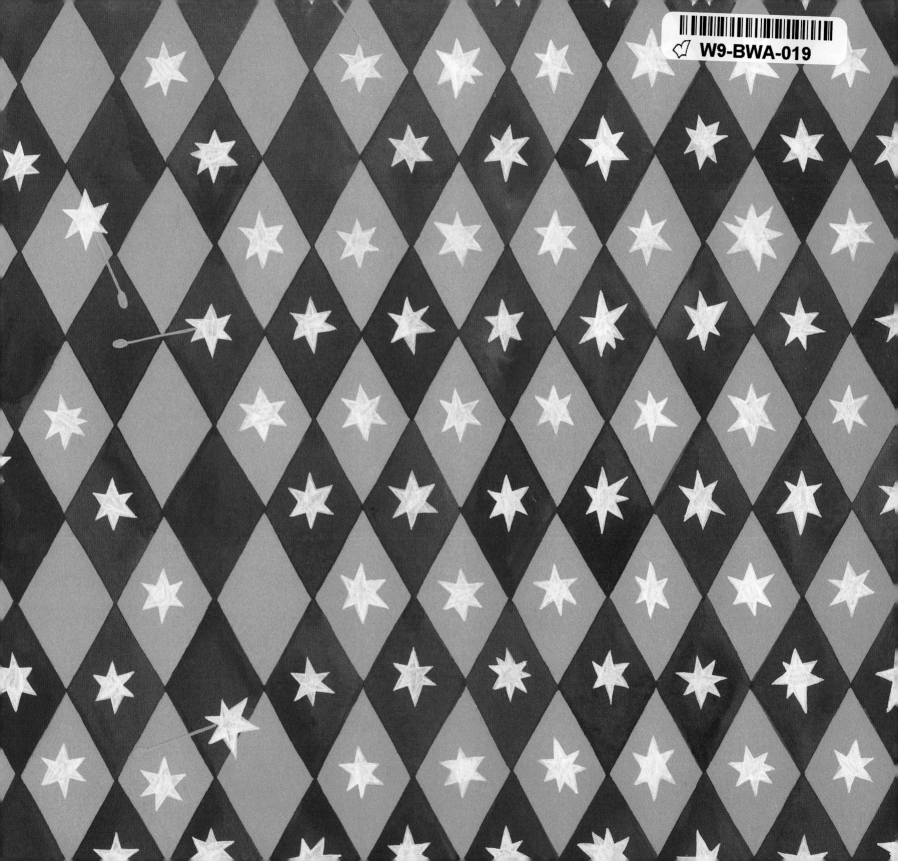

Night Wishes

Poems selected by
LEE BENNETT HOPKINS

Illustrated by
JEN CORACE

EERDMANS BOOKS FOR YOUNG READERS

Grand Rapids, Michigan

For Charles, who made all my wishes come true.

— L. B. H.

Contents

Bed

Rebecca Kai Dotlich

Climb in, child.
Climb in.

Cuddle into thoughts
of things you did today.

You ran, splashed, slid,
skipped, roamed, raced.
You pedaled, waded, wandered.

Now—
pull your blankets close
up tight
as I warm your sleep
throughout the night.

Climb in, child.
Climb in.

Pillow

Matt Forrest Esenwine

What dreams might wait for us tonight?
What might you do?
    What might you see?
Will open skies draw you to flight?
    Who might you meet—or be?

Perhaps you'll dig through ancient sands,
discover dynasties of old,
or travel interstellar lands
for treasures yet untold.

Eyes closed, set sail!
Until the morn,
imagination's winds will blow.
Your mind is where adventure's born,
    so come, my child . . .
        . . . let's go!

Blanket

Jude Mandell

At bedtime, when it's time to rest,
you grab me tightly—
nuzzle,
nest.
Curl in closer,
with a tug—
a happy,
"love my blankie" hug.

All cuddled up and sleepy-eyed,
you
jelly-roll
yourself
inside.
Snuggle
warm,
the long night through . . .

Sweet dreams, Dear One.
I love you, too.

Cat

Eileen Spinelli

Let's watch the moon swim
through sleepy sky
and nod to night owl's call nearby.
Let's dream together,
you and I.

I'll dream of sunlit fisheries
with daring things to do.
You'll dream of starry wisheries
where sweetest dreams come true.

Think of this, dear little one—
wouldn't it be fine
if you found me in your dream?

If I found you in mine?

Dog

Irene Latham

You're sleepy-still.
Your breathing's deep. . .

Remember the day we dug a hole?
Played chase with the surf?
You gathered seashells
while I spun in happy-yappy circles.

When blazing sun and burning sand
made our eyes start to blur,
we curled together under
a wide, striped umbrella.

You are my runner, my snuggler,
my best-ever fetch-er.
Are you dreaming now—like I am—
about our next adventure?

Clock

Prince Redcloud

Tock
    tock
broken clock.

My tick
is gone.
  Tock
      tock.
No need to fix me.

There is time
to put
my tick
back in.

Maybe tomorrow.

I can wait.
So can you.
It takes a lot of
tick-tock
    tick-tock
    tick-tock
    tick . . .

to grow.

Rocking Horse

Alice Schertle

Hurry up, sun!
Hurry up, dawn!
Light up the sidewalks,
the bushes,
the lawn.

Shine in the window,
light up the room.
Shiny new morning,
wake her up soon.

Alone I can't gallop,
can't canter, can't walk,
but when she is with me—
together
      we rock!

Book

Joyce Sidman

Snug on your shelf,
not far from your bed,
I am the book your papa
just read.

A colorful story,
a twist, a surprise,
that drifts through your head
and softens your eyes.

Night melts your room
into shadows and ink.
Think of my pages,
O Dreamer,
just think. . .

As you slide into sleep
in the darkness that clings,
I'll quietly wait
like a bright stack of wings.

Teddy Bear

Lee Bennett Hopkins

I have been
kissed, hugged
tossed, thrown—

my clothes
are tattered,
there are
knots in
my fur . . .

but
I don't care.

I'm here for you
to snuggle into
as you
squeeze me tight

until
tomorrow's
morning
light.

Angel
Nikki Grimes

Sleep, child.
Sleep.
No need to fear the dark
while I stand guard.

I'll softly kiss your eyelids,
and fill your dreams
with sweetness,
with light.

Stars

Deborah Ruddell

Out in the stillness
we twinkle away,
listening closely
to hear what you say.

Tell us your wishes
and close your eyes tight.
No need to hurry—

we listen all night.

Moon

Darren Sardelli

I am the moon,
I light the night
with threads of silver,
gold, and white.

I send my beams
of love and light
to you, my child,
with great delight.

While snuggled soundly
safe in bed,
my magic glistens
overhead.

Night-light
Renée M. LaTulippe

Nighttime falls—all is still—
I begin to glow.
My soft blue light illuminates
things I love and know.

There's Train, asleep upon his tracks.
Doll snoozes by your door.
Xylophone rests upon a chair,
while Blocks doze on the floor.

But one thing I love most of all—
you there, curled up tight.
As dreamtime settles over you,
I glow my sweet goodnight.

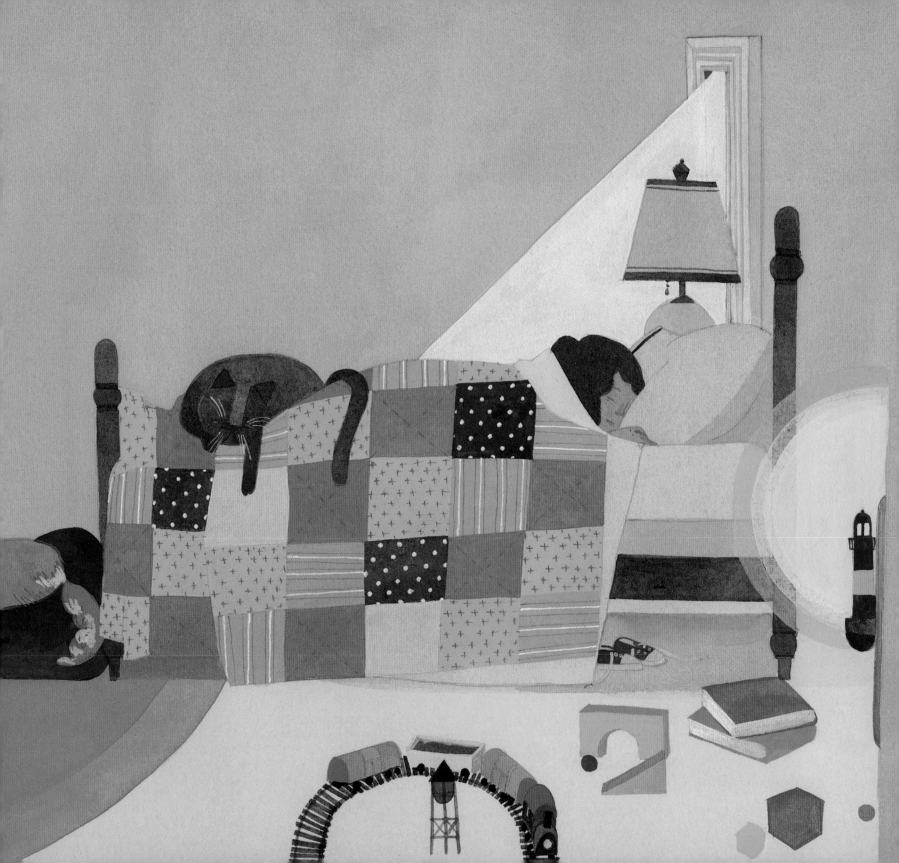

Bed Again
Rebecca Kai Dotlich

Climb out, child.
Climb out.

Rub eyes, yawn, stretch.
Roll out from my warm place.

Tuck covers in for now.
Step out and into day.
Get dressed, be on your way.

Do all those things again,
race, roam, wander.

Climb out, child.
Climb out.

Time to learn all there is to know.
Grab your breakfast,
your curiosity,
your wonder—

and go.

ACKNOWLEDGMENTS

Thanks are due to Curtis Brown, Ltd. for use of "Bed" and "Bed Again": copyright © 2020 by Rebecca Kai Dotlich;
"Angel": copyright © 2020 by Nikki Grimes; "Teddy Bear": copyright © 2020 by Lee Bennett Hopkins;
"Night-light": copyright © 2020 by Renée M. LaTulippe; "Clock"; copyright © 2020 by Prince Redcloud.
All used by permission of Curtis Brown, Ltd.

Thanks are also due for commissioned works used by permission of the respective poets who control all rights:
"Pillow" by Matt Forrest Esenwine; "Dog" by Irene Latham; "Blanket" by Jude Mandell; "Stars" by Deborah Ruddell;
"Moon" by Darren Sardelli; "Rocking Horse" by Alice Schertle; "Book" by Joyce Sidman; "Cat" by Eileen Spinelli.

Illustrations © 2020 Jen Corace

Published in 2020 by Eerdmans Books for Young Readers,
an imprint of Wm. B. Eerdmans Publishing Co.
Grand Rapids, Michigan

www.eerdmans.com/youngreaders

Manufactured in China

28 27 26 25 24 23 22 21 20   1 2 3 4 5 6 7 8 9

Library of Congress Cataloging-in-Publication Data.

Names: Hopkins, Lee Bennett, editor. | Corace, Jen, illustrator.
Title: Night wishes / poems selected by Lee Bennett Hopkins ; illustrated
    by Jen Corace.
Description: Grand Rapids, Michigan : Eerdmans Books for Young Readers,
    2020. | Audience: Ages 4-8. | Summary: "Featuring fourteen poems by
    multiple authors, this anthology imagines how clocks, teddy bears, and
    other bedtime companions say good night"— Provided by publisher.
Identifiers: LCCN 2020002177 | ISBN 9780802854964 (hardcover)
Subjects: LCSH: Children's poetry, American. | Bedtime—Juvenile poetry. |
    CYAC: Bedtime—Poetry.
Classification: LCC PS586.3 .N544 2020 | DDC 811/.60809282--dc23
LC record available at https://lccn.loc.gov/2020002177

Illustrations created with gouache.